THE MYSTERY OF THE WILD WEST BANDIT

created by
GERTRUDE CHANDLER WARNER

ALBERT WHITMAN & Company
Chicago, Illinois

Library of Congress Cataloging-in-Publication Data

Warner, Gertrude Chandler, 1890-1979.
The mystery of the Wild West bandit / by Gertrude Chandler Warner ;
interior illustrations by Anthony VanArsdale.
pages cm. — (The Boxcar children mysteries ; 135)
Summary: "The Aldens are at Wildcat Crossing, a recreated frontier
town full of cowboy fun. But when horses disappear and other pranks threaten
to ruin the Wild West show, the Boxcar Children must find out who's
the varmint causing all the trouble"— Provided by publisher.
ISBN 978-0-8075-8725-6 (hardback) — ISBN 978-0-8075-8726-3 (paperback)
[1. Mystery and detective stories 2. Brothers and sisters—Fiction. 3. Orphans—
Fiction. 4. Wild west shows—Fiction.] I. VanArsdale, Anthony, illustrator. II. Title.
PZ7.W244Mxqt 2014
[Fic]—dc23   2013033072

J\

The Mystery of the Wild West Bandit
Created by Gertrude Chandler Warner

10 9 8 7 6 5 4 3 2 1 LB 18 17 16 15 14 13

Cover art by Logan Kline.
Interior illustrations by Anthony VanArsdale.

For more information about Albert Whitman & Company,
visit our web site at www.albertwhitman.com.

Contents

THE MYSTERY OF THE
WILD WEST BANDIT

CHAPTER 1

A Wild West Ride!

"Next stop, Wildcat Crossing," said the announcer.

"We're almost there!" said Benny. The six-year-old boy pressed his nose against the train window. He watched the Texas desert scenery race by.

"And we're right on time," said Benny's fourteen-year-old brother, Henry. He glanced across the aisle at Jessie, who smiled. The two older siblings had a secret they were keeping from their young siblings. Their little sister, Violet, who was ten, was sleeping peacefully next to Benny. Watch, their wire-haired terrier, dozed at Jessie's feet.

The Alden children were riding on the Lone Star Flyer, a train that ran through parts of the American Southwest. Their grandfather had put them on the train in El Paso that morning. They were going to spend a few fun days at the annual Wild West Festival. It took place in a town called Wildcat Crossing.

Jessie gently nudged Violet. "Let's get our bags so we'll be ready to get off the train," she said. Jessie was twelve and often acted motherly toward her two younger siblings.

"I was dreaming about our boxcar!" Violet said, smiling and rubbing her eyes.

"The train makes me think of our boxcar, too," said Benny.

At one time, the Alden children had lived in an old railroad boxcar in the woods. Their parents had died, and they had run away instead of going to live with Mr. Alden, their grandfather. They had heard that he was mean, but he turned out to be really very nice. Happily, he found his grandchildren and brought them to live with him. He even moved the boxcar to his backyard in Greenfield.

"I think we're here," said Henry. The train slowed down and came to a gentle stop.

"Wildcat Crossing," said the announcer. "Welcome to the Wild West!"

"Okay, let's get our bags and go!" said Jessie. She and Henry grabbed their suitcases and herded the younger children to the exit. They were the only passengers who got off the train.

"Wow, look at that!" said Benny.

The children saw a wooden wagon with a big palomino horse harnessed to it. The horse and wagon stood in the road next to the little train station. A friendly looking bearded man sat in the front seat of the wagon.

"Howdy, partners!" he said, smiling. "My name is Bart. Trigger and I have been waiting for you!"

Trigger nodded his head up and down and snorted.

"We're going to ride in a real horse-driven wagon?" asked Violet. Her eyes were open wide.

"That's right," said Henry. "Grandfather arranged for his friend Bart to pick us up in true Wild West style." Henry extended his hand to Bart. "I'm Henry. Thank you for meeting us!"

"It's my pleasure," said Bart, shaking Henry's hand.

"Wow!" Benny said again.

"We're so glad to meet you, Bart," said Jessie. She introduced her sister and younger brother and they all climbed into the wagon.

"Wildcat Crossing is not far from this stop," said Bart. "We'll be there in no time." He made a clucking sound and Trigger set off at a slow trot.

"Look at all the cacti," said Jessie as they bounced along.

"I see yellow, orange, and red flowers on some of them," said Violet. Violet loved nature and pretty things. She pulled a camera from her bag and took photographs.

Benny put his hand over his eyes to shield them from the bright sun. "Look!" he said, pointing. "That's a huge rabbit out there! It's bigger than Watch!"

The children watched as a jackrabbit loped across the scrubby terrain. Watch yipped.

"Their big ears help them stay cool in the hot weather," said Henry. Henry had been reading about the Texas desert in preparation for their trip. "They can also run very fast, up to forty miles an hour."

"That's right," Bart said from the front seat. He guided Trigger through an open gate next to a large parking lot. A small group of cattle with huge horns watched them go by from a fenced area nearby. "And jackrabbits eat cactus—imagine that!"

"Yikes, that would hurt to eat those sharp thorns," said Benny. "Are those your cows?" he asked.

"Those are real Texas longhorn cattle," said Bart. "They're here for the festival."

The children gasped as Wildcat Crossing appeared ahead of them.

"This town looks just like a Western movie!" said Violet.

"We think it looks better than a Western movie," said Bart. He helped the children out of the wagon. Then a large man with a curly mustache and black hat walked up. He led Trigger and the wagon down the road without saying a word.

"Don't mind Jack McCoy," said Bart. "He's always grumpy like that. We just ignore him."

"Hello there, Aldens!" said a friendly voice. "I'm Nellie, Bart's wife and partner." A tall woman wearing a long striped dress with a bright blue apron stood in the doorway of a building. "Come on in and have a snack."

"We're happy to meet you," said Henry.

"We're happy to meet you and have a snack!" said Benny.

Jessie patted Benny's head and laughed. "This is Benny, Henry, and Violet, and my name is Jessie," she said. "Benny is a bottomless pit when it comes to food."

"That's okay with me," said Nellie, smiling.

"We always have plenty of food at Wildcat Crossing. Cowboys love to eat too!"

"S-a-l-o-o-n," said Benny, reading the sign over the door of the building. "What is a saloon?"

"This saloon is a Western-style restaurant," said Bart. "It has food, drinks, and entertainment. Come on in!"

The children followed Bart and Nellie inside the saloon. Nellie introduced them to Calamity Connie, her sister. Connie was placing menus on the tables.

"I'm pleased to meet you," said Calamity Connie. "I hope you enjoy the festival!"

"I love your shiny pink boots!" said Violet.

"Thank you," said Calamity Connie. "I love pink—and purple too!"

"So do I!" said Violet. "Purple is like my name, Violet."

"What does *calamity* mean?" Benny asked.

"Calamity means disaster. It's the stage name that Nellie gave me," said Connie. She scowled at her sister, who smiled.

"It's all in fun," said Nellie. "Connie

is a very talented musician. It's just that sometimes…"

Just then Connie dropped the pile of menus, which scattered all over the floor.

"See?" said Nellie.

"I'm a clumsy gal," said Calamity Connie with a laugh. The children helped her gather up the menus.

Then everyone enjoyed fresh biscuits with scrambled eggs, cheese grits, and glasses of milk. When they were finished, Bart took the Aldens up the road to the bunkhouse where they would be staying.

"We've known your grandfather since Nellie's parents built this town," said Bart. "I'm glad he let you come visit! You'll have lots of fun."

"Thank you," said Jessie. "We're also here to help in any way we can." The children nodded in agreement. They liked to chip in and help people.

"Oh, don't worry, we'll keep you busy!" Bart promised. "Okay, get settled and then feel free to wander around. We'll have lunch back at the saloon at twelve. But watch out, you never know what might happen in the meantime." He winked and smiled then left.

"I wonder what he meant by that," Violet said. She looked nervous.

"You'll see. Don't worry," said Henry. Jessie smiled with him.

"Oh, another surprise!" Benny said. "I love Wildcat Crossing! It's full of surprises."

The children unpacked their clothes and headed back outside. They wandered along the wooden sidewalks, peering in the windows of the old buildings. There was a huge museum with lots of Western history and a library filled with old books. They also noticed a stable for horses near a big outdoor stage. There were hitching posts for horses all along the lane. One horse, a sleepy back one, was hitched to a post by the saloon.

When they had seen every building, the Aldens ventured back to the saloon to see if Connie needed any help with lunch.

"Oh, you're back," Connie said, appearing

at the kitchen doorway. Her face was red and she was out of breath. Violet noticed that her shiny pink boots looked a little dusty.

"We came to see if you needed any help," said Jessie. "Are you okay?"

"I'm fine, and I don't need any help right now," said Connie. "Why don't you tour the town?" Connie didn't wait for an answer. She ducked back into the kitchen.

"I guess she doesn't need any help," said Violet. The children went back outside.

"Look at that big stage," said Henry, pointing at the large structure in the center of the town. "This must be where they have the stage shows for the festival." They admired the ornate wooden building. It had a big red velvet curtain in front.

"There's a sign," said Benny. "It says *Wildcat Stage*." Benny was just learning to read and liked to practice by reading signs.

"We'll be helping with the stage play tomorrow," said Violet. "I can't wait! I'm going to take lots of pictures."

"I wonder where everyone is," Jessie said.

"It seems like a ghost town. Earlier we saw people walking around."

Suddenly a man with a bandana hiding most of his face rushed out of a building. It had a sign that read *bank*. The masked bandit leaped onto the black horse tied to the hitching post by the saloon. The bandit galloped down the road. Clouds of dust billowed in his trail. Bart, dressed in a black suit, ran out of the bank.

"*Stop, thief!*" yelled Bart.

Nellie appeared in the bank window wearing a colorful costume. "*We've been robbed!*" she screamed.

A cowboy on a white horse galloped in from behind the big stage. He was dressed in a fancy white and gold outfit. "Somebody call Sheriff Dooworthy!" he yelled. His horse circled in the dirt.

A woman wearing a shiny star on her plaid shirt appeared from a building marked jail. "*Hey!*" she yelled. "Somebody stole Tricky Trigger!"

Bart, Nellie, and the cowboy all stared at her.

"Wait a darn rawhide minute," said Bart. "That's not in the script!"

CHAPTER 2

Trigger Is Missing

The Aldens rushed to join the frantic group. The man playing the part of the masked bandit returned. He jumped off his horse. Then he removed the bandana, smoothed his curly mustache, and scowled. "What the heck happened?" he asked.

"That's the grumpy guy," whispered Benny.

"Yes, that's Jack McCoy," Henry whispered back.

Everyone else was talking at once.

"Everyone, please, calm down," said Bart. "Wanda, what happened?"

"Trigger wasn't tied up behind the jail where he was supposed to be!" Wanda waved her arms around as she talked. She glared at Jack McCoy. "You were supposed to make sure Tricky Trigger was ready for rehearsal!"

"Don't look at me," Jack griped. "I had Trigger tied up where he belonged. And I had Blackie out there by the saloon. I waited in the bank for my cue. I did my job."

"What's a cue?" Benny whispered.

"Shh," Jessie replied. "We'll tell you later."

"I didn't see anything," said the cowboy in the white-and-gold suit. "I was behind the stage waiting for my cue."

"You're always waiting for your cue, Dapper Dallas," said Jack. He sneered at the fancy-dressed cowboy.

"Cut that out, boys," said Nellie. "We have to find Tricky Trigger. That horse is worth a fortune. It looks as if somebody may have stolen him."

"You're in charge of the horses, Jack," said

Wanda. "So you must know where Trigger is."

"Well contrary to what you think, Sheriff Wanda Dooworthy, I sure don't know," said Jack. "So maybe we should look for that valuable horse." He got back on Blackie. He headed up the road, dust clouds trailing behind them.

"Oh dear," said Nellie, watching the dust roll by. "What next?"

"It's just a coincidence, Nellie," said Bart. He patted her arm. "Trigger probably just got loose and Jack is embarrassed. We'll find him."

"Has something else like this happened?" Henry asked.

"This is not the first mishap," said Bart. "Just the other day—"

"We aren't going to find Trigger by standing around here yakking," said Dapper Dallas, interrupting. "Hey, you kids, do you know how to ride a horse?"

"You bet we do!" said Jessie.

"And we want to help find Trigger," said Henry.

"Come on then. Let's saddle up," said Dallas. "Let's go, Wanda!"

Bart and Nellie stayed behind in case Trigger wandered back to town while the Aldens and Wanda followed Dallas to the stable. The Aldens donned cowboy boots, and then Wanda, Henry, and Jessie saddled up on their horses. Violet and Benny got to ride twin ponies named Mutt and Jeff.

"Hurry up, please," said Wanda. "Trigger is smart enough to find his way back home, but not if he's in trouble."

The group headed down the lane past the stage and the saloon. They trotted down the road that the children had traveled earlier. Everyone looked around, hoping to spot Trigger.

"I wonder where Jack McCoy went," Jessie said, trotting alongside Wanda.

"He might be ahead of us or he may have circled back the other way," said Wanda.

"Jack sure is grumpy," said Benny. He and Violet rode their ponies next to each other.

Wanda sniffed. "Jack is a grump all right.

He's worse than ever since I got his job playing the part of sheriff in our shows."

"Why did he lose the job?" Henry asked.

"Because he was taking it too seriously," said Dallas. "Always telling everyone what to do. So Bart took it away from him."

"And now he gets to be a bad guy and take care of the horses," said Wanda. "It seems to suit him."

Benny looked down at Dallas's bright blue sneakers. "Don't cowboys wear boots to ride horses?" he asked. Benny pointed to his own cowboy boots.

Henry noticed that Dallas frowned and then smiled. "Well, sure, little partner, but the boots I wear are very expensive. I want to keep them clean and shiny for our performances."

"Oh, okay," said Benny.

Suddenly Mutt, Violet's pony, whinnied. "Mutt, what's the matter?" asked Violet. Mutt looked around nervously as he walked.

"Maybe he heard something," said Jessie.

"Hold up, everyone," said Wanda.

"Did you hear that?" asked Dallas. He turned his horse back toward Wildcat Crossing and put one hand up to his ear. "That was a horse whinny!"

"Maybe that's what Mutt heard," said Violet. "Oh, I hear it too!"

"I hear it too. It sounds like Trigger," said Wanda. "Let's go!" She spurred her horse and galloped back toward Wildcat Crossing.

"Come on, kids!" yelled Dallas. "Yee haw!" he sang as he followed Wanda back down the road.

Henry, Violet, and Benny turned to follow, but Jessie raised her hand to stop them.

"Wait. I think the sound came from down the side road we just walked by," she said. "Dallas and Wanda may have heard another horse at the stable in town."

"Wanda might be too upset to recognize Trigger's voice," said Violet.

"You two could be right," said Henry. "Let's sit quietly for a minute."

The children waited quietly, their horses staying still and silent.

"There it is again!" said Benny. It *is* coming from that side road!" He walked his pony down the narrow drive. Jessie followed along with Violet and Henry. The road looked like nobody had used it for a long time. Tree roots split the pavement and grass grew in the cracks. Desert willow branches hung down so that the children had to duck to get past them.

Benny's pony, Jeff, whinnied just as they approached an old wooden building that looked like a barn.

"I don't see Trigger," said Violet, looking around. "Mutt, where is Trigger?"

Mutt snorted and grabbed a mouthful of grass by the road.

"Mutt doesn't seem upset anymore," said Henry. "Maybe we're close to Trigger."

"Let's ride around to the back of the building," suggested Jessie.

They walked their horses around the barn. They were greeted by a nicker and a snort.

"Hello there, Trigger!" said Henry. "We've been looking for you."

The big palomino horse nodded his head and whinnied. He was inside the old barn with his head hanging out an open window. He wore the bridle and saddle that Jack had put on him earlier.

"Thank goodness he's okay," said Violet. She jumped down from her pony and walked over to greet Trigger. He nuzzled her hand and pawed the ground.

"Let's get him out of there," said Jessie. She got off her horse and pulled open a big door. Trigger happily clopped out and Violet grabbed his reins.

"What's that taped to his saddle?" Benny asked.

Violet reached for the bright orange piece of paper taped to Trigger's saddle and handed it to Benny. "I don't think I can read this," he said.

Henry walked his horse over to help. Benny handed him the piece of paper and Henry read the note aloud for everyone.

"*Sell Wildcat Crossing or else...Trigger will disappear for good!*"

"Look at the swirly *r*s!" said Benny.

"Look at the purple ink!" said Violet.

Just then Jack McCoy appeared riding Blackie. "There you are!" he said.

CHAPTER 3

Interested Parties

"Wanda and Dallas thought Trigger was back at Wildcat Crossing," Henry explained. "But we tracked his whinnies to this old barn."

Jack trotted Blackie over to Trigger and took his reins away from Violet. "I'll take our boy home," he said. Before the children could say anything more, Jack McCoy headed up the road with Trigger in tow.

"He really is grumpy," said Violet. "We didn't even get a chance to tell him about the note."

"Maybe Bart is right. He's just embarrassed," said Jessie. "Or maybe he has something to hide. Let's tie up our horses and see if we can find any clues."

"Good idea," said Henry. "Maybe we can figure out who stole Trigger and wrote this note." He put the note in his pocket.

"There are hoof prints here," said Jessie. "They lead into the barn through the door."

The children crept inside the old barn, following the footprints.

"Look, here are boot tracks. They go this way," said Henry. The children followed the boot tracks to the big double doors on the front of the barn. Henry shoved open the doors that led to the road. The tracks continued outside and toward the road.

"It looks as if whoever took Trigger rode him here, walked him in through the back door, and then ran away on foot!" said Violet.

"And they were wearing boots," said Benny. "Jack McCoy was wearing boots. But Dallas wasn't."

"Those are good clues, Benny," said Henry.

"Calamity Connie was also wearing boots," said Violet. "They were dusty."

"And she was out of breath when we saw her just before the rehearsal," said Henry.

"Can we tell how big the boots are from the tracks inside the barn?" asked Henry. "That might help to figure out who they belong to."

They studied the boot tracks. They were all mixed up with the hoof prints from Trigger stomping and pawing the ground.

"We can't tell much from these prints other than they have heels and are shaped like cowboy boots," said Jessie. "We can't really tell how big they are."

"Let's go back to Wildcat Crossing and talk to Calamity Connie," said Henry.

* * *

The Aldens steered their horses to the stable near Wildcat Stage. Jack McCoy was outside with Trigger, brushing him and muttering.

"Wanda the whiner...she doesn't know how to play the part of sheriff. Whoever heard of a lady sheriff anyway? Have you, Trigger? I sure haven't."

"Hello!" said Henry, not wanting to eavesdrop.

The other children got off their horses and greeted Jack.

"Where have you kids been?" he grumbled. "I need to get ready for tomorrow."

"We're sorry," said Jessie. "We were trying to figure out who moved Tricky Trigger."

"That's just history," said Jack. "Right now you need to groom, water, and feed your horses."

"We will!" said Violet. "Thank you for letting us ride them."

"Yes, thank you!" said Benny. "It was a fun ride and we're glad we found Tricky Trigger."

Jack grunted something and put Trigger in his stall. He showed the children where to put their saddles and bridles. Then he stalked toward the saloon.

"Oh well," said Jessie. "Jack is grumpy as usual. Let's take care of our horses and then go to the saloon."

"Did you hear him complaining about Wanda?" asked Violet. "It sounds like he's pretty mad about her getting his acting job."

"That's right," said Henry. "But is he grumpy enough to try to hurt the Wild West Show by hiding Tricky Trigger?"

"The note said to sell Wildcat Crossing or Trigger would disappear forever," said Benny. "What did that mean?"

"I don't know," said Henry. "We need to learn more about those past troubles Bart mentioned."

The children carefully groomed their horses. Then they put them in their stalls where fresh hay and clean water were waiting for them.

"I guess Jack really does care about the horses," said Violet. "He made sure they have their lunch."

"Let's go to the saloon and have lunch too!" said Benny.

The children walked down to the saloon. They heard loud voices as they approached.

"I told you we are not selling Wildcat

Crossing! Quit coming around here and bugging us about it!" Bart was yelling at a man in a suit standing in front of the saloon. There was a bright yellow car parked in the middle of the dirt road. Benny noticed that the man was wearing cowboy boots.

"And get that car out of here," said Bart angrily. "We don't allow cars in Wildcat Crossing. You were supposed to park in the parking lot outside of town!"

"I'm sorry that I didn't know about that rule," said the man. "I meant no harm, it's just that..."

"Just nothing, get in your car and get gone!" Bart yelled.

The man climbed into the car. He leaned out the window as Bart stomped toward the saloon. "I know you're going to change your mind. I'll be back!"

"And I'll run you off again," Bart mumbled. The children joined Bart as he stomped inside.

"Hey, Aldens, thanks so much for finding Tricky Trigger!" Bart said, brightening a little.

"You're welcome," said Henry.

"Who was that man?" asked Benny. "You seemed very cross with him."

"Benny, that's not our business," said Jessie.

"It's okay, Jessie and Benny," said Bart. "That was Jasper Beebe, a real estate agent. He's been coming around here a lot lately."

"Hello there, children," Nellie said, waving them to a table where she was sitting. "I hear you found our prize trick horse!"

"Yes, thanks to Mutt!" said Violet.

"Violet, I'm sure you had something to do with it too," said Nellie. "Here, have some chili. Connie made us a big batch along with her homemade cornbread."

The children sat down and enjoyed the chili and cornbread.

"Why does Jasper Beebe want you to sell Wildcat Crossing?" asked Jessie.

Nellie and Bart exchanged a look. "Jasper has a client that wants to use Wildcat Crossing as a movie set," explained Nellie as Bart scowled.

"Nellie's parents set up Wildcat Crossing

to honor history," said Bart. "They didn't like the way Hollywood made up stories about the West. They wanted to be true to the American West, and that's the way we are today."

"We saw the museum and the library," said Henry. The other children nodded. They could tell that Bart and Nellie felt strongly about their Wild West town.

"But that Jasper Beebe never seems to give up," said Bart. "And he seems to show up whenever anything goes wrong."

Henry looked at his brother and sisters but stayed quiet.

"What happened last time Jasper was here?" Jessie asked.

"Someone poured salt into our water tower," said Nellie. "The next day while we were trucking in water from El Paso, Jasper showed up trying to convince us to sell the town."

"I think you need to see what we found taped to Trigger's saddle," said Henry. He pulled the orange note out of his pocket and handed it to Bart and Nellie.

They read the note and Bart shook his head. "I don't trust that Jasper Beebe any farther than I could toss him, but he just got here. He even parked his car in the middle of the road," he said. "Trigger was stolen over two hours ago."

"Maybe he was here earlier and nobody saw him," Jessie suggested. The children told Bart and Nellie about the boot prints they found earlier at the barn.

"Jasper Beebe was wearing cowboy boots," said Benny. "I saw them."

"Well, that is interesting," said Bart. He handed the note back to Henry.

Violet was very quiet. She had noticed that Jack McCoy was sitting across the room, watching them intently.

CHAPTER 4

A Musical Motive?

The next morning was the first day of the Wild West Festival. Jessie and Henry got dressed and helped Violet and Benny put on their Western outfits too. They would be participating in the show and wanted to look the parts.

"We look just like real cowboys!" said Benny.

"And cowgirls," said Violet, smiling. She wore a purple shirt, blue jeans, and purple boots. "I can't wait to show Calamity Connie my purple boots!"

"We can also talk to Connie about yesterday," said Henry.

"Good idea," said Jessie. "I wrote notes in my notebook last evening after you had gone to sleep."

"What do we know so far?" asked Henry.

Jessie flipped through the pages in her notebook. "We know that whoever stole Trigger was wearing cowboy-style boots. Connie, Jack, and Mr. Beebe were all wearing cowboy boots yesterday," she said. "Dallas was wearing sneakers, so we can rule him out."

"He said he likes to keep his expensive boots clean," said Benny.

"That's right, Benny," said Henry.

Jessie continued. "Calamity Connie was out of breath when we visited her just before the rehearsal," she said. "Did she hide Trigger at the old barn and then run back just as we got there?"

"Why would she want Wildcat Crossing to be sold?" asked Henry.

"Maybe we can find out by talking to

her," said Violet. "I can talk to her about our colorful boots!"

"That's a good idea, Violet," said Jessie. "She might tell you about more than her boots."

"Okay, I can't wait!" Violet was excited. She liked to help when she and her siblings were trying to solve a mystery.

"And then there's Jack," said Henry, smiling at Violet. "Jack was supposed to tie up Trigger, but who would have seen him do that?"

"Everyone else was waiting for their cues," said Benny. "I figured out that a cue means a signal to do something," he said proudly.

"That's right, Benny," said Henry. "And we know that Jack is jealous of Wanda. Maybe he just wants to make trouble for Bart and Nellie."

"He is awfully grumpy," said Benny.

"He was glaring at us yesterday during lunch," said Violet. "He looked mad."

"And Jack had time to ride Trigger to the old barn and run back to the bank," said Henry. "Just like Connie."

"What about Jasper Beebe?" asked Violet.

"He is another suspect," said Henry. "We learned that he wants the town to be sold."

"And Nellie said he seems to show up right when something bad happens," said Jessie.

"It seems that we have a lot to find out!" said Violet.

"That we do!" said Henry. "And now, we're going to a Wild West Festival!"

They headed to the saloon where Connie, Bart, and Nellie were making breakfast.

"You're just in time!" said Nellie, waving at the children as she turned bacon and stirred sausage on a huge iron grill. "We expect about a hundred people for breakfast!"

The gate to Wildcat Crossing would open to the public at ten o'clock. The children had promised to be at the saloon early to help with the cooking and preparation.

"Benny and I can make the biscuits," said Jessie.

"Thank you," said Nellie. "The biscuit dough is right there in that bowl." She pointed to a huge ceramic bowl that was filled with a large pile of biscuit dough. "Just put flour on your hands, pinch off a little bit of dough, shape it into a biscuit, and put it on a baking sheet."

"And set the timer!" said Benny.

"That's right, Benny," said Nellie. "We don't want burned pinch biscuits!"

"I can help make the pancakes," said Henry.

"Thank you, Henry," said Bart. "But around here we call them flapjacks!" Bart laughed as he and Henry began pouring batter onto a griddle in small puddles. Soon the flapjacks bubbled.

"I'll help Connie set up the tables," said Violet. Jessie smiled as Violet headed outside to where tables and chairs had been set up.

"Hi, Connie," Violet said, seeing Connie putting tablecloths on one of the tables. "May I help you?"

"Yes indeed!" Connie. "You're Violet, right?"

"That's me," said Violet. "Thank you for remembering my name!"

"It helped that I noticed your purple

cowboy boots," laughed Connie. "They are very pretty."

"Thank you," said Violet. She took a tablecloth from a pile nearby and spread it over a table.

Connie came over and helped Violet smooth out the cloth.

"How long have you worked here?" Violet asked.

"All my life, it seems," said Connie. "And I can't afford to leave unless Bart and Nellie sell it. I would get some of the money since our parents owned it."

Violet was quiet for a moment. She didn't want to pry too much. "Where would you go if you had the money?" she finally asked.

"If I had the money, I would go to Nashville," said Connie. "I want to pursue my music career. Playing here for the shows isn't enough anymore." Connie grabbed a pile of silverware from a table and dropped it all on the ground.

"Oh shoot, there I go again." Connie sighed.

"It's okay, I didn't mean to upset you," said Violet. She helped gather up the silverware and went to the kitchen for clean replacements.

"Is everything all right?" Jessie asked her in the kitchen.

"Connie needs clean forks and knives," said Violet. "She seemed upset talking about

wanting to leave Wildcat Crossing. Then she dropped a pile of silverware!"

Jessie gathered up more silverware and put the pile in a basket. "This should work for Calamity Connie," she said, smiling. "Did you find out anything?"

"Yes, I did," said Violet. "But I need to take this basket to her. I'll tell you later!"

Violet rushed back outside and joined Connie. They finished setting the tables without any more mishaps. Violet enjoyed talking to Connie. She didn't like to think of her as the bandit who took Trigger.

"Thank you for all your help, Violet," said Connie. "And look, here comes the crowd!"

Bart had opened the gate. Visitors were arriving and sitting down at the outside tables. Henry, Jessie, and Violet raced to help serve flapjacks, bacon, sausage, and biscuits to everyone. Benny stayed busy bringing everyone fresh pots of warm gravy. Bart and Nellie collected money and poured hot cups of coffee.

There was too much excitement for Violet

to get a chance to tell her siblings about what Connie had told her.

Suddenly the door to the jail burst open and Jack McCoy appeared. He was wearing his black hat and had on a black shirt and jeans. This time he wasn't wearing a mask. His curly black mustache waved in the breeze.

"Yeeeee haw! I'm a free man!" he yelled.

The visitors applauded as Jack jumped onto Blackie who was tied to a hitching post nearby. He spurred Blackie and left a plume of dust as he whooped and galloped up the road.

Just then Dapper Dallas appeared in the jail doorway. He was dressed in jeans and a plaid shirt. "That bandit Jack McCoy just escaped from jail! Somebody call Sheriff Dooworthy!"

Wanda, who had been sitting with the visitors, jumped up from her table. "Here I am!" she yelled. She ran over to Tricky Trigger, who was also tied up near the jail. She leaped onto the horse from behind, landing neatly in his saddle. The crowd whooped at the fancy trick.

Trigger reared up and waved his front legs, his white mane blowing in the breeze, prompting more applause.

"I'll get that no good, trouble-making bandit!" Wanda yelled. She spurred Trigger to gallop after the disappearing Jack, dust billowing behind her.

Everyone stood, clapping and cheering. It was the beginning of the Wild West Show!

CHAPTER 5

A Nervous Performer

Wanda and Trigger soon reappeared. Trigger nodded his head and swished his tail as he walked to the front of the stage. Wanda held Blackie's reins. Jack McCoy hung his head from atop Blackie. His hands were tied with rope and he was scowling.

"He looks grumpy as usual," said Benny.

"He does make a great bad guy," said Jessie. "He can just be himself!"

"I bet he doesn't like that Wanda is the one who caught him!" said Violet.

Dapper Dallas walked up and took Blackie's reins. "Good job, Sheriff Wanda Dooworthy!" he said. "You caught this no-good bandit."

He steered Jack and Blackie toward the stable. The crowd applauded as Jack was led away.

"Let's go, Benny," said Henry. "That was our cue to head backstage to help set up."

Henry and Benny hurried to the backstage door. Trigger pranced to the center of the road and whinnied. As the crowd gathered along the road, Wanda stood up in her saddle and waved. Then Trigger cantered past the audience with Wanda balancing on one leg. Several people gasped when Wanda leaned backward and performed a handstand before sitting back in the saddle. She guided Trigger over to where the crowd stood clapping.

"Gather around, everyone!" she said. "Meet Tricky Trigger, the smartest horse in the Wild West!"

Trigger lowered his head and bowed. Then he pawed the ground and whinnied again.

"Wow!" said Violet. "Trigger is a very smart horse!"

"Come on, Violet," said Jessie, "That was our cue!"

"I'm a little scared," said Violet. "There are a lot of people watching."

"It'll be fine," said Jessie. She knew that Violet didn't like big crowds. "I'll be with you the whole time."

Violet took a deep breath. "Okay, let's go!" she said.

The two children walked out to where Wanda and Trigger were waiting.

"Ladies and gentlemen," said Wanda, "Trigger will now give this pretty girl a kiss!"

The audience chuckled as they watched the fun.

"Jessie, please tell Tricky Trigger that you would like a kiss!" said Wanda.

Jessie leaned close to Trigger. "Give me a kiss, please, Tricky Trigger," she said. She giggled as the big horse smooched her on the face. The crowd laughed and clapped.

"You have now been smooched by a horse, Jessie!" said Wanda. "How did you like it?"

"It tickled!" said Jessie, wiping her face and smiling.

"Tricky Trigger is a wonderful kisser," said Wanda. "But he is also very smart. He can answer questions." Wanda waved to Violet. "Violet, would you please ask Tricky Trigger a question?"

Violet stepped up close to Trigger. She took another deep breath.

"How old are you, Tricky Trigger?" Violet asked.

Trigger seemed to think for a few seconds. Then he stomped the ground ten times.

"Tricky Trigger says he is ten years old," said Violet.

"That's right! Trigger is ten years old— just a little kid!" said Wanda.

"He's the same age as me!" said Violet. She smiled and petted Trigger on his soft nose.

The crowd laughed and applauded again. Jessie looked past everyone and noticed Dapper Dallas duck behind the big stage. Then she spotted Jasper Beebe. He was walking into town from the direction of the parking lot. She noticed his silky white suit and shiny tan cowboy boots.

Wanda had Trigger turn and nod to the audience.

"Hello there, sir," said Wanda to Jasper. "Come on over here. Tricky Trigger wants to ask you a question."

Jasper glanced around, looking confused. People in the crowd urged him to play along. Finally he walked slowly to where Trigger stood with Wanda, Violet, and Jessie.

"Jasper looks scared," whispered Violet. "He is shaking and his face is all shiny."

"I wonder why he's so scared," whispered Jessie.

Just then Tricky Trigger reached over to Jasper and snatched his big white hat. Jasper screeched and took several steps backward. He almost knocked over a woman standing behind him. The crowd laughed. Trigger handed the hat to Violet. She took the hat to the still quivering Jasper.

"Here you are, Mr. Beebe," she said.

"Thank you, my dear," said Jasper. Then he retreated quickly into the crowd.

"Enjoy the show, everyone!" said Wanda. "And let's give a cheer to our helpers—Jessie and Violet Alden!"

The crowd applauded as Jessie and Violet waved and smiled.

Then the red stage curtain rippled. Dapper Dallas appeared and bowed to everyone. Dallas was now dressed in a sparkling sequined black and red suit. He wore black boots with silver buttons and a big red cowboy hat.

"Dapper Dallas sure changed his clothes quickly," Jessie said. "We just saw him wearing jeans and a plaid shirt."

"Maybe he's a quick-change artist, like in a magic act!" said Violet.

"He is a fast changer, that's for sure," said Jessie.

"Ladies and Gentlemen, your attention please!" said Dapper Dallas. "Let's give Tricky Trigger and Wanda a big hand. It's time for our stage show to begin."

The crowd cheered and applauded some

more. Wanda led Trigger behind the stage, waving good-bye. Trigger pranced and swished his long white tail.

"I think Trigger likes the applause!" said Violet. Jessie smiled at her little sister. Violet loved animals. She liked to see them loved in return.

The audience sat down in the chairs facing the stage. They watched Dallas as he strutted across the stage.

"We have a special treat for you today," said Dallas. "We have a little lady who can sing like a bird. Her cowboy ballads will bring you to tears, I promise." Dallas took off his hat and stepped to the side of the stage. "Ladies and gentlemen, I present to you: our very own...Calamity Connie!"

Dapper Dallas disappeared from the stage as Connie appeared from between the red curtains. She wore a glittery silver and pink outfit that matched her pink boots. She had on a big pink cowboy hat. There was a guitar strapped to her shoulder.

"She looks beautiful!" said Violet. "I can't

wait to hear her sing! I hope Henry and Benny can hear too."

"Henry and Benny are backstage, not very far away," said Jessie. "They'll be able to hear Connie sing."

Dallas reappeared with a stool and a microphone. Connie tripped as she sat down on the stool. Members of the audience gasped as she almost fell off the stage.

"Don't mind me, folks," Connie laughed nervously. She scrambled to sit down. "Now you know why they call me Calamity Connie!"

The audience laughed with her. Dallas placed the microphone stand in front of Connie's stool. Then he left the stage without a word.

"She looks kind of nervous," said Jessie. "I wonder what's wrong."

"Maybe she's scared to be in front of all these people," said Violet. "That's how I would feel."

"You were great with Trigger," said Jessie.

"Trigger made me feel safe," said Violet. "I

could forget the crowd."

"Animals can do that," said Jessie.

Calamity Connie settled on the stool. She strummed her guitar. The audience became quiet.

"I hope you all know the words to 'Home on the Range,'" said Connie. She began to sing and play. The audience joined her. By the time everyone got to the last verse, Connie had a lot of fans. She sang lots of audience favorites. The whole town filled with songs like "Streets of Laredo" and "Oh, My Darling Clementine," led by Connie's voice. When the last song ended, Connie tuned her guitar nervously. She looked back at the closed curtain.

"Bravo, Calamity Connie!" yelled Jasper Beebe. He stood and applauded louder than anyone else. The rest of the crowd stood up and kept clapping. They started chanting for more songs.

Connie kept looking back at the curtain.

"She seems more nervous than ever," said Jessie.

"I wonder what's wrong," said Violet. "Everyone loves her. She should be happy!"

Just then, Bart walked over from the side of the stage and whispered something to Connie.

"Oh no!" Connie cried. "I wondered what was going on back there!" Connie leapt from her stool and ducked back between the curtains. Her stool clattered to the floor. The microphone stand teetered for a few seconds.

"Everything's okay, folks," said Bart. "The show will continue in a moment or two." He grabbed the stool and ran behind the curtain.

"We should go see what happened!" said Violet. "Henry and Benny might be in trouble!"

Jessie and Violet raced around to the backstage door.

CHAPTER 6

More Trouble!

Jessie and Violet found Henry and Benny backstage. Costumes were scattered all over the floor. Henry, Benny, and Nellie were trying to sort through them. Jessie and Violet knelt down to help.

"Where is my costume for the play?" Connie cried. She surveyed the mess of clothes. "I have to change right away!"

"And I can't find the pajama top I'm supposed to wear," said Bart.

"Here is your nightshirt, Bart," said Nellie.

She handed him a big blue shirt.

"That's not it, but it will have to do," said Bart. He grumbled as he headed off to a curtained dressing room.

"Is this your dress, Connie?" Violet held up a pink striped dress.

"Yes, thank you, Violet!" Connie took the dress and raced away.

"Where is my sheriff's shirt with the badge?" cried Wanda. "I can't be the sheriff without my badge!"

"Here it is, Wanda," said Benny.

"Thank you, Benny!" she said. "Someone please tell Jack I'll be there in a second. He's with Trigger right outside." She ran to another dressing room.

Jessie peeked out the backstage door. She saw Jack holding Trigger. "Wanda will be here soon," she said.

"What's going on in there?" Jack asked.

"Someone tossed all the costumes on the floor and mixed them up," said Jessie. "Did you see anyone go in here earlier?"

"Nope," said Jack. "My job is to open and

close the stage curtains. And I take care of the horses. I don't have time to see what anyone else is doing." He looked away. Jessie walked back inside.

"Does everyone have their costumes?" asked Henry.

"I think so," said Nellie.

Henry surveyed the piles of clothes, shoes, hangers, and hats. "What a mess," he said. "We should clean this up for you."

"We can clean this up later," said Nellie. She sighed and shook her head. "This isn't fun anymore," she said softly.

Dapper Dallas appeared, wearing a black suit and black hat and boots. "What happened here?" he asked.

"Someone is having fun with us again," said Nellie. "Although Bart and I don't think it's much fun."

Dallas looked around and smiled. "Well, I'm sure glad that my clothes were already in my dressing room!"

He walked over to a bulletin board with a sign on top that said *Today's Scenes*. It had colorful notes tacked all over it. The Aldens watched as he grabbed a bright yellow note from the middle of the board and read it. Then he pinned the note back to the center of the board.

Bart, Connie, and Wanda came out of their dressing rooms. "We're as ready as we'll ever be," said Bart.

"As they say in Broadway, the show must go on!" said Dallas. "Let's go, actors, it's show time!"

Connie took her place at the piano. Bart got into a bed on the stage and pulled up the covers. Nellie sat in a chair next to the bed. She brought out a handkerchief.

"Is everyone ready?" asked Dallas.

"Yep," said Bart.

"Ready," said Nellie.

Connie waved.

"Okay, kids, skedaddle to your seats," said Dallas. "And wait for your cue."

"What does *skedaddle* mean?" Benny asked as the children headed to the front of the stage.

"It means hurry up!" said Jessie, laughing. "I'll tell you how to spell it later."

The red curtains rippled again. Dapper Dallas appeared. "Greetings once more, ladies and gentlemen," he said, bowing. "Allow me to introduce myself."

The curtain slowly opened. Piano music floated out from the stage.

"My name is Dastardly Dallas," growled Dallas with an evil sneer. "When it comes to money, I always get what I want."

The curtain opened wide. The stage revealed Connie at the piano. Her fingers raced over the piano keys as she played. In the center of the stage, Nellie sat by the bed. She held the handkerchief to her mouth and sobbed. Bart was propped up on pillows. He looked very weak and sick.

"Is Bart okay?" Benny asked.

"Bart is okay, Benny. Remember that this is a melodrama," said Jessie. "Melodramas exaggerate everything."

"That's right," said Henry. "And Bart is just acting."

"I remember what you told me," said Benny. "A melodrama is a play!"

"It's just make-believe," said Violet. "But Bart is a good actor!"

"He is!" said Benny. "I thought he was really sick."

The play began. Violet took her camera out of her pocket and took pictures. Dallas approached Nellie and Bart. "Pay the rent!" he yelled. He pointed his finger at them.

"But we already paid the rent!" said Nellie. "Please, can't you see? My husband is very sick!"

"You may have paid the rent," said Dallas, "But I raised the rent!" He sneered again and laughed.

"You raised the rent last month!" cried Nellie. "We can't afford to pay you more rent!"

"Pay the rent, or I will *throw you out*!" yelled Dallas.

"Please, have mercy," said Bart. He lifted his head from the pillows. Then he fell back with a loud moan.

Nellie hugged Bart. "Oh, please, is there someone out there who can save my poor sick husband and me from Dastardly Dallas?" she cried.

"That's our cue!" said Henry. The Aldens stood up and started to boo and hiss.

"Dastardly Dallas, you are not a nice man!" yelled Violet.

"You won't get away with your dastardly deeds!" yelled Benny. He smiled. He was happy that he remembered his big line in the play.

"Good job!" whispered Jessie. "Sheriff Dooworthy, where are you?" she yelled.

"Oh no, not Sheriff Dooworthy!" said Dallas. He looked around, looking afraid. "She will take me to jail!"

"You should go to jail," said Nellie. "You are dastardly in your deeds!"

"Dastardly!" yelled the audience. They were on their feet. Connie was banging on the piano keys. Her loud music added to the angry mood.

"I think I hear the clopping of horse hoofs," said Henry. "Help is coming!"

"Hurray! Here comes Sheriff Dooworthy!" said Jessie.

Wanda appeared on the stage riding Tricky Trigger. Trigger clopped across the stage. He nodded his head and snorted.

"Yay, Tricky Trigger!" yelled Violet and Jessie. "Get that Dastardly Dallas!"

The audience joined in the cheers. Wanda jumped off Trigger. She put her hands on her hips. "Your days of terrorizing tenants are over, Dastardly Dallas!" she said.

Dallas hung his head and put out his hands. Wanda wrapped his hands with rope. Then she tied the rope to Trigger's saddle horn.

"Let's go to jail," said Wanda. She hopped back onto Trigger and led Dallas off the stage.

The audience cheered.

"Thank goodness for Sheriff Dooworthy!" said Nellie. She kissed Bart on the cheek. The curtain closed.

The audience applauded. The curtains opened again and Nellie and Bart stood and bowed. Connie stood and bowed with them. Then Wanda reappeared with Trigger. They both bowed to cheers. Finally Dallas appeared, waving and smiling. He took off his hat and bowed.

"Dapper Dallas seems to like being the star," said Jessie.

"Yes, he does," said Henry.

Violet was studying the curtain. "How does the curtain open and close?" she asked.

"That's Jack's job," said Jessie. "He told me earlier that he's in charge of closing and opening the curtains."

"Where is Jack now?" asked Benny.

"I think he's outside waiting for Trigger," said Henry.

"He doesn't get any applause for his work," said Violet. "That's sad."

"I guess it is sad," said Henry. "But is he the one pulling the pranks?"

"He is grumpy," said Benny.

"But he loves animals," said Violet. "People who love animals are good."

Jessie gave her sister a hug. "You might have a point there, Violet," she said. "We'll see if we can figure out who is causing Bart and Nellie so much trouble."

Dallas, Bart, Nellie, and Connie had climbed off the stage. They visited with the audience. Wanda brought Tricky Trigger around to join them. Trigger bowed for people to stroke his neck. Dallas signed autographs while Bart and Nellie talked to visitors.

"Look," said Jessie. "I see Connie outside the saloon. She's talking to Jasper Beebe."

The children watched as Connie shook hands with Jasper Beebe. She looked over at the Aldens then ducked into the saloon.

"I wonder what they were talking about," said Jessie.

"Let's see if we can find out," said Henry. "It's time to help get lunch ready."

CHAPTER 7

Barbeque, Sarsaparilla, and Questions

The audience and other visitors explored Wildcat Crossing and enjoyed the sites and activities. Jack had pony rides set up for children. Wanda showed off her trick roping skills to the delight of a small crowd. Dapper Dallas's voice boomed as he told stories about the Old West. Some people visited the historic museum and library.

The Aldens headed to the saloon. They had work to do.

"There's Connie," said Jessie. "She's already hard at work."

"Hey there, Aldens," said Connie. "I'm putting barbeque beef on homemade rolls. I need someone to wrap them up, please."

Henry and Violet washed their hands and helped wrap sandwiches into paper.

"I can run the cash register," said Jessie.

"Thank you!" said Connie. "Nellie is busy at the souvenir shop and Bart is busy in the office."

Jessie took money from a line of customers. Henry and Violet handed them their wrapped sandwiches.

"Benny, you can give people their drinks!" said Connie. She showed Benny the cooler and put him to work.

Benny handed each person a cold bottle of sarsaparilla from the cooler. He had fun explaining what Henry had told him about the spicy old-fashioned drink. "It's made from sarsaparilla roots and licorice," he explained to each customer who wondered. "It's kind of like root beer."

Jasper Beebe appeared near the end of the line of hungry customers. Violet noticed that Connie looked away when it was his turn to pay for his food.

Soon the line was much smaller. "It looks like we have plenty of sandwiches wrapped up to sell," Connie said to Henry and Violet. "You should eat too!"

"And I can take over the cash register," said

Nellie, putting on an apron. "Bart's running the souvenir shop."

"Thank you," said Jessie.

"I'm ready to eat," said Benny. "And have my very first sarsaparilla!"

Connie put four sandwiches on a tray along with napkins. "Benny will get your drinks!" she said, smiling.

"I don't think I can carry that many!" said Benny.

Henry grabbed the tray while Violet helped Benny carry bottles of sarsaparilla. They headed toward an empty table near Jasper Beebe.

Jasper saw the children approaching. He waved them to sit in the empty chairs at his table. "Please, join me," he said, smiling.

"Maybe we can find out what he and Connie were talking about," whispered Jessie. The children smiled and joined Jasper Beebe at the table.

"Thank you for inviting us to join you," said Henry. He introduced his brothers and sister.

"Connie told me about you," said Jasper. "She said your grandfather is an old friend of Bart and Nellie."

"That's right," said Henry. "Grandfather was friends with Nellie and Connie's parents when they first built Wildcat Crossing."

"We're here to help!" said Benny. "We're having a cattle drive this afternoon."

"I wondered why those big longhorns were in the paddock by the parking lot," Jasper said. "That will be, uh, interesting."

Violet noticed that Jasper looked nervous, like he had when he was close to Tricky Trigger.

"Wildcat Crossing has sure come a long way," said Jasper, wiping his brow. "I've been trying to convince Bart and Nellie that they can make money if they sell it."

Violet noticed Connie looking at them. She wondered if Connie could hear their conversation.

Jasper looked over at Connie and she ducked into the kitchen.

"I don't think that Bart and Nellie want to sell Wildcat Crossing," said Jessie.

Jasper leaned close and whispered, "Connie really wants to sell it," he said. "She told me so this afternoon. She is part owner!"

"Bart doesn't want the spirit of Wildcat Crossing to get lost," said Benny.

"Why would that happen?" asked Jasper.

"Because it would be fake like a Hollywood set," said Violet. "Wildcat Crossing honors the Old West."

"You children seem to know a lot about Wildcat Crossing," said Jasper. "My buyer wants to honor the Old West, just as Bart and Nellie do," he said.

"That's not what it sounds like to Bart," said Henry. "He asked you to leave and said that he would never sell."

"Well, maybe you children can convince him," said Jasper. "Please tell Bart and Nellie that my buyer is not like Dastardly Dallas."

"We're just guests of Bart and Nellie," said Jessie. "We don't want to pry into their business.

"That's right," said Henry. "But we would

like to help find out who the bandit is that keeps making trouble for them."

"Do you know anything about that?" Jessie asked.

"Why, yes," said Jasper. "Connie told me about the trouble that's been happening here."

"Bart and Nellie are very upset about it," said Henry. "Especially the threat to steal Tricky Trigger!"

"Oh my," said Jasper. "I thought they were all just harmless pranks!"

"The note said Trigger would disappear forever if they didn't sell Wildcat Crossing!" Benny blurted.

Jasper looked up sharply. "That is terrible," he said. "Um, may I see the note?"

Henry pulled the note from his pocket and unfolded it for Jasper.

Jasper peered at it and looked troubled. "I know nothing about any of it." He gathered up his empty sarsaparilla bottle and the paper from his sandwich. "It was very nice visiting with you," he said. Jasper Beebe headed for the saloon door.

"He acted like he knew something," said Jessie.

"He seemed upset about the threat to make Trigger disappear," said Violet.

Henry was thinking. "That's true. He thought the mishaps were harmless pranks until Benny told him about the note."

"I'm sorry," said Benny. "Was that supposed to be a secret?"

"It's okay," said Jessie. "I'm glad you mentioned the note."

"He seemed to change when he saw the note," said Henry.

"He left really quickly after that," said Violet.

"What are you all so serious about?" Nellie came over and sat down in Jasper's vacant chair. She had a barbeque sandwich and a bottle of sarsaparilla. "I noticed you were talking to that pest, Jasper Beebe."

"Yes," said Violet. "He was very nice until we showed him the note about Tricky Trigger."

"That is interesting. I don't trust that man," said Nellie.

Just then Connie screamed.

"Oh, for pity's sake, now what?" Nellie cried. She and the children raced to the kitchen.

Connie was standing in the middle of the kitchen. "Oh shoot, I'm sorry," she said. "There was one of those horned toads under the kitchen sink. It scared the spit out of me!"

"You grew up around lizards and snakes," said Nellie. "You used to have a horned toad for a pet! What is wrong with you lately?"

"It's nothing," said Connie. "I'm sorry to scare everyone."

"Where is the horned toad?" asked Benny. "I'd like to see it!"

Connie laughed. "I scared the poor thing back through the hole in the wall," she said. "But you can spot them in the desert all the time if you look very carefully."

"Okay," said Benny. "I'll look for one!"

Just then Dapper Dallas yelled from outside the saloon. "Clear the road, everyone! Cattle coming through."

"That's our cue!" said Benny. The children said so long, raced back to their table, cleaned up their mess, and headed outside. It was time for the cattle run!

CHAPTER 8

The Round Up!

The tourists gathered along the sidewalk as Henry, Jessie, Violet, and Benny ran to the stable. Wanda let Tricky Trigger entertain the crowd. Dallas busied himself riding up and down the street. He announced the upcoming cattle drive and waved. Violet noticed that he was wearing a new outfit. This one was a flashy black and yellow shirt and pants and a yellow ten-gallon hat. His boots were bright yellow.

When the Aldens arrived at the stable,

Jack McCoy was grumpier than usual. "I've been waiting for you kids," he griped. "I had your horses saddled up thirty minutes ago. I couldn't leave them."

"We're very sorry," said Henry. "Thank you for waiting for us!"

"Get going so I can get back to my chores," said Jack. He helped Benny and Violet get on Mutt and Jeff as Jessie and Henry mounted their horses.

They thanked Jack again. Then they trotted their horses over to Wanda and Dallas.

"Here we go!" yelled Dallas. He spurred Blackie and raced past the crowd. Wanda followed on Trigger, and the Aldens galloped their horses to keep up.

"Yee hawwwww!" Dallas yelled. He whooped as they galloped up the road.

But when they got to the paddock, the gate was open. The cattle were gone. Dallas circled Blackie around the fence. He shaded his eyes with his hand and looked around.

"Looks like that bandit got our dogies!" he said.

"Dogies?" asked Benny.

"Sure, partner," said Dallas, laughing. "Get along, little dogies!" He trotted Blackie to the big parking lot, looking around.

"It's another word for cows," whispered Jessie.

"This is bad," said Wanda. "We borrowed ten Texas longhorn cattle just for the festival. They are worth a lot of money."

"We must find them!" said Jessie. "Bart and Nellie don't need more trouble."

"Look," said Violet. "There's a piece of yellow paper taped to the fence."

"I'll get it!" said Benny. He rode Jeff across the muddy paddock and grabbed the note. "It looks like the same purple handwriting as before," he said. "But I need help to read it." Benny rode over to Jessie and handed her the note.

"It says, *Sell Wildcat Crossing now or things will only get worse for you!*" said Jessie. "The handwriting looks the same as the other note."

"The swirly *r*!" said Benny. "That's what I saw too."

"Oh dear," said Wanda. "These threats are getting more serious."

Just then Dallas reappeared. "I can't find them anywhere. I'll tell Bart and Nellie what happened. You all can look for the cattle."

Dallas raced back down the road without another word.

"He was sure in a hurry," said Henry. He put the note in his pocket.

"He seemed almost happy that the cattle were missing," said Violet.

"Dallas loves drama," said Wanda. "He thinks he's an actor. Come on, let's track down those cattle. Hopefully they were just set loose and not trucked away."

They noticed hoof prints coming out of the open gate and followed them up the road.

"There are no tire tracks," said Henry. "So maybe someone just opened the gate."

"Let's hope so!" said Wanda. They rode their horses along the road, following the prints.

"I think you're all good actors," said Benny. "The show was fun!"

"You children did a great job," said Wanda. "You got the audience involved."

"You seem to love Trigger," said Violet.

"Yes, he's my buddy," said Wanda. "I always look forward to working with him at the festival. The rest of my life is not that exciting!" She laughed.

"What does everyone do when they aren't working at Wildcat Crossing?" asked Jessie.

"Jack is a construction foreman, which might be why he's so bossy," said Wanda. The children giggled. "Dallas is an aspiring actor who plays in his community theater. Otherwise he works at a tire store. Me, I drive a city bus."

The cattle tracks turned down the same dirt lane that led to the old barn. Wanda and the Aldens steered their horses to the lane.

"So you see, we have a lot of fun doing this in our free time each year. It's exciting and different."

"Connie says she is stuck here," said Violet.

"That's right," said Wanda. "She lives and works here all year, managing the museum, souvenir shop, and restaurant with Bart and Nellie. She wants to pursue her music career but can't do that from this faraway place."

"That's sad," said Violet.

"Hey, look," said Benny. "Are those our cows?" He pointed at some cattle grazing in the distance.

"They are cows, that's for sure," said Wanda. "Let's get a closer look."

They guided their horses closer. "Yep, I see the star brand and those telltale long horns."

"One, two, three, four, five, six, seven, eight..." Benny counted. "...Nine, ten!" he said. "That's all of them!"

* * *

The tourists applauded as Wanda and the Alden children herded the cattle into town.

Dallas appeared on Blackie. "Okay, everyone, let's continue with the show," he said.

"We're ready," said Wanda.

The children all nodded. They took their places around the ten cows, keeping them still.

"You can see how the famous Texas longhorn cow gets its name," he announced. "These amazing creatures are related to the first cattle ever brought to the United States."

The audience admired the huge twisted horns on the cattle.

"Now Miss Wanda and Trigger will show you how we cut a cow away from the herd," said Dallas.

Wanda and Trigger separated one of the cows from the group. Then she let Trigger's reins go. Trigger leaned left and then raced right as the cow tried to rejoin its herd.

"As you can see," continued Dallas, "Tricky Trigger is also a mighty fine cutting horse!"

The audience applauded as Wanda and Trigger herded the cow down the road. The cow stopped and Trigger kept it from running back. Finally Wanda pulled up Trigger's reins, allowing the cow to rejoin its family. The cow raced back, mooing and shaking its head.

"That cow is glad to be back with its friends," said Benny.

"She sure is," said Jessie.

"We cut a cow for different reasons," said Dallas, "like when it needs medical attention. It's all part of the cattle drive." He nodded to Wanda as she rejoined the group. She nodded back.

"Driving cattle is an Old West tradition," said Wanda. "Cowboys on horseback moved huge herds of cattle from their pasture to the market."

Dallas walked toward the little herd as Wanda talked. The children divided up on either side of the herd. Benny stayed behind with Dallas. The longhorns looked around and started walking.

"Millions of them were herded for hundreds of miles," Wanda said. "They only walked a short distance each day. They didn't want the cattle to lose weight. So a cattle drive could take a very long time!"

The Aldens and Dallas slowly circled the little herd back up the road to where the audience stood.

"That's right, Wanda," said Dallas.

"The famous Chisholm Trail was almost a thousand miles long. It took the cowboys over two months to make the trip."

"So, children, are you ready to drive these cattle?" asked Wanda, smiling.

"We're ready!" said Benny. Wanda and Dallas stood back as Henry, Violet, Jessie, and Benny coaxed the little group of cattle back up the road. The audience applauded and cheered.

"Dallas sure takes his acting seriously," said Jessie.

"Yes, he seems to enjoy the many roles he plays," said Henry.

They saw Jack McCoy standing at the gate of the paddock. "Bart says we better lock them up until we know who's messing up things around here," he said. He kicked at a pile of fresh hay nearby. The cattle went rushing into the paddock, splashing mud and dirt. Jack shut and locked the gate with a chain and padlock.

"Nice job," he said, brushing his muddy jeans. "I'm going to town for some supplies.

Do you remember how to put away your horses?"

"Yes," said Henry. "We'll take care of them, don't worry."

Jack snorted as he stomped over to a truck in the parking lot. The children watched as he drove away. They noticed that Jasper Beebe's car was gone. They walked their horses back to the stable.

"He said nice job," said Jessie. "We've never heard him say anything that kind."

"And he trusted us with the horses," said Violet. "I don't think Jack McCoy is a bandit."

"He's just a grump," said Benny.

"I'm not sure," said Henry. "Jack had time to hide Trigger and mess up the costumes. And he may have put salt in the water tower. We weren't here for that."

"But we also saw him take Tricky Trigger to the stable after the show," said Jessie. "Jasper said that he saw the cattle when he got there just as the show started."

"Jack had to saddle up our horses and then stay with them until we got there," said Henry.

"Plus he had to open and close the curtains during the play and take care of Trigger," said Violet. "He was too busy to be the bandit!"

"I don't think Jack is the bandit," said Henry.

"Jack is just a grumpy man who loves horses," said Violet. She smiled.

"We still have other possible bandits," said Jessie. "I just hope we can find out who it is before things get worse."

CHAPTER 9

Fancy Handwriting

The children passed a few visitors heading back to their cars. The people were smiling and talking. Several waved as the children rode by. "Nice job! Thank you!" said one man. Henry, Jessie, Violet, and Benny waved and smiled.

"We had a wonderful time in Wildcat Crossing," said a woman. She held hands with two little children. They all smiled and waved at the Aldens.

"Not everything went wrong today," said Jessie.

"We had lots of fun!" said Benny.

"If we can figure out who the bandit is, then it will be a perfect day," said Henry. "We still have work to do."

Back at the stable, the children removed saddles and bridles from their horses. They put the items into the tack room. Then they carefully groomed their horses. They spotted Trigger nodding from his stall. Wanda had already come and gone.

"Who is the possible bandit now?" Jessie asked. "We decided that Jack isn't the bandit."

"I'm glad that the bandit isn't Jack," said Violet. "And I like Calamity Connie too."

"Connie wants to sell Wildcat Crossing," said Henry. "She doesn't like being stuck here."

"She could have moved Trigger," said Jessie. "Remember how she was out of breath?"

"That's true," said Violet. "And she likes purple. The notes were written in purple ink." Violet sighed.

Jessie slowly brushed her horse and thought. Suddenly she remembered something.

"Connie was on stage, in the audience, or in the saloon all day. We saw her," she said. "She was never muddy or dusty. Whoever let loose the cattle would have gotten dirty."

"That paddock is awfully muddy," agreed Henry. "But Connie could have slipped backstage and changed her clothes," said Henry.

"And messed up the costumes at the same time," said Jessie.

Violet thought of something. "Wait! Do you know who changes clothes quickly?"

Her siblings looked at her, confused.

Then Jessie nodded. "Dapper Dallas!" she said.

"Yes!" said Violet. "He disappears and reappears in a new outfit very fast!"

"That is interesting," said Henry. "We didn't think Dapper Dallas was the bandit. He wasn't wearing cowboy boots when Trigger was taken."

"But he changes clothes very quickly," said Jessie.

"And shoes," said Violet.

"But it doesn't make sense," said Jessie. "Why would Dallas want to sell the town to a Hollywood producer? He seems to love his job here." She brushed her horse's mane as she talked. "I think Jasper Beebe could be our bandit. He showed up right after Trigger was taken."

"He keeps showing up whenever there is trouble," said Henry. "That's what Nellie and Bart said."

"And he was here when the costumes were messed up," said Violet. "We saw him."

"His suit was very clean," said Jessie. "I don't think he let the cattle out or he would be muddy."

"Unless he changed clothes," said Henry.

"There were a lot of costumes backstage that anyone could use," said Jessie.

"And they could hide the muddy clothing," said Henry. "I'm not sure being muddy is a good clue."

"I know a good clue," said Benny. He was quietly brushing Jeff and listening to his brother and sisters talk.

"What's your clue, Benny?" asked Violet.

"Jasper Beebe wouldn't take Trigger. And he wouldn't let out the cattle," Benny declared.

"Oh, you're right!" said Violet. She clapped her hands.

"What is it, you two?" Henry asked.

"Jasper is afraid of horses!" said Benny. "Violet told me. He screeched when Tricky Trigger took off his hat."

"Jasper is afraid of cattle too, I think," said Violet. "He got nervous just talking about them and he left before the cattle drive started!"

Jessie and Henry patted Violet and Benny on their backs. "You're right. That definitely rules out Jasper Beebe as our bandit," said Jessie. "Good job!"

"So we're left with Calamity Connie," said Henry.

"And Dapper Dallas," said Jessie. "I think I know why he could also be our bandit. Remember who the buyer is?"

"A Hollywood producer," said Henry.

"Maybe Dallas told the producer he could convince Bart and Nellie to sell," said Jessie. "Maybe they promised him an acting job if he was successful."

"He might do anything to make that happen," said Henry.

"We now have two possible bandits," said Jessie. "Where do we go from here?"

"I think we need more clues," said Benny. The other children agreed. They put their horses into their stalls and gave each horse fresh hay and water. Then they walked back to Wildcat Stage.

The children entered through the back door. Costumes were still strewn on the floor. Nobody was around.

"Oh goodness! We forgot to clean up this mess," said Violet.

"We were busy!" said Jessie, laughing. "We can clean it up now."

Henry and Jessie picked up hangers, dresses, shirts, pants, and jackets and hung them on the costume racks. Benny collected shoes and boots and found their matches.

Violet helped Benny line up the shoes and boots under the costume racks. They had the mess cleaned up in no time.

Violet pointed to the bulletin board. "Look at the different colored notes here," she said. There were lots of notes tacked to the board. The notes were blue, pink, yellow, and orange.

"I think the orange and yellow notes are the same size and color as the notes we found."

"I have them in my pocket," said Henry. He brought the two notes out. Then he held them up to the bulletin board. "Yes, they are!" he said.

The children studied all the notes on the board. The notes seemed to have handwriting of all kinds. "Here is one that used purple ink!" said Violet.

Henry reached for the note she pointed to and inspected it. "It's hard to tell if the same person wrote this note," he said. "Look, Benny, there are no *r*s to compare." He showed the note to Benny.

"What about the one that Dapper Dallas read before the play started?" asked Benny.

"I remember that note," said Violet. "I watched him tack it in the middle after he read it."

Henry reached for the bright yellow note in the middle of the bulletin board. "It looks like it has lines for the part of Dastardly Dallas," he said.

"Dastardly Dallas said, 'Pay the rent!'" said Benny. "What does the *r* look like?"

Henry smiled as he showed Benny the note.

"There is a swirly *r*, just like in the other two notes!" said Benny.

"It looks as if Dapper Dallas is our dastardly bandit!" said Jessie.

"Maybe not," said Henry. "We don't know that Dallas wrote this note."

"Oh, that's right," said Jessie. "Maybe someone else wrote the note for him. It could have been Connie."

"We know that Connie loves purple," said Violet.

"Look, there's a pad of paper on the table over there," said Benny. He ran over to inspect his find. He held up the colorful pad of paper. The other children joined him.

"There's a pen here too," said Jessie. She picked up the pen from the table. She scribbled on the pad of paper. "It has purple ink!"

"Anyone could have written the notes with that pen," said Violet. "It was here for everyone to use." She seemed relieved.

"You're right, Violet," said Henry. "We need to figure out a way to trap the bandit. I think we know that it's either Calamity Connie or Dapper Dallas."

"That's right," said Jessie.

"And I have an idea," said Violet. She looked at her brothers and sister proudly. "I think I know how we can find out which one is the bandit."

"How can we do that?" asked Jessie.

"With their help!" said Violet.

CHAPTER 10

The Bandit Is Revealed!

"Please tell us your idea, Violet!" said Benny.

"Yes, please," said Henry. "How are we going to find out who is the bandit?"

Violet took her camera out of her pocket. "I've been taking photos of all the actors," she said. "See, they're in a collection I made called Wildcat Crossing."

Violet showed the photos she had saved on her camera.

"You did a nice job taking photos!" said

Jessie. "There's Bart acting in the play. And there is Nellie bending over him."

"Here is Calamity Connie playing guitar. And Dallas acting as the evil landlord!" said Violet.

"Look, there's Wanda riding Tricky Trigger. And Jack McCoy playing the part of the bank robber," said Benny.

"What do these photos have to do with figuring out which one is our bandit?" asked Henry.

"What do actors do with photos of themselves?" Violet asked, smiling.

"Oh!" said Jessie. "They autograph them!"

"What a great idea, Violet," said Henry. "We can ask Connie and Dallas to autograph their photos."

"Then we can check to see who has the swirly *r*," said Benny. Then he thought of something. "Dallas and Connie don't have an *r* in their names." Benny frowned.

"You're right, Benny," said Henry. "You're getting very good at spelling!"

Benny grinned.

"We'll ask them to sign it 'at Wildcat Crossing' after they write their names," said Jessie.

"*Crossing* has an *r*!" said Benny.

"Good idea!" said Violet. "Now we just need to print the photos."

"Maybe Bart has a printer in his office," said Jessie. "Let's see if he's there."

"My camera can plug into a printer," said Violet. "I brought the cord with me. It's in our bunkhouse."

The Aldens raced up the road to the bunkhouse. They retrieved the cord for Violet's camera, and they went back to the saloon. Connie was sitting by herself at a table. Nellie was working at the cash register. No one else was around.

"Hey there, Aldens," said Nellie. "Thanks for finding those cattle! Did you get them put away without any trouble?"

"Yes," said Henry. "Jack McCoy put a chain and a padlock on the gate."

"Bart told him to," said Nellie. "We're so tired of all the problems we've been having.

Maybe we should just give in and sell the town."

Nellie noticed that Benny was hopping from one foot to the other. "Benny, what's wrong?" she asked him.

"We know who the bandit is!" whispered Violet. Benny nodded his head up and down.

"But we have to prove it," whispered Jessie. The children glanced at Connie. She didn't seem to hear what they were saying.

"Is Bart in the office?" asked Henry. "We want to ask him something."

"Yes, just down the hall across from the kitchen," said Nellie. She followed the children to the office.

"Good to see you," said Bart. He was sitting at a chair behind a desk stacked high with papers. "I'm just sorting through the mess. What can I do for you?"

"We'd like to print two photographs," said Henry. "We think we know how to identify the bandit!"

"Is that so?" asked Bart. Henry, Jessie, Violet, and Benny took turns telling Bart and Nellie what they had learned. They showed them the notes and explained that the handwriting was the final clue.

"You kids are darn good detectives," said Bart, smiling. "So it's either Nellie's sister Connie or Dapper Dallas?"

"That's right," said Jessie.

"I hope it's not Connie," said Nellie. "She should have told us if she was unhappy." Nellie frowned.

"We'll find out who it is," said Bart. He came from behind the desk and gave Nellie a hug. "And we'll go from there, Nellie. Okay, Violet, let's plug your camera into the printer."

Violet and Bart hooked up the camera. They printed out a photo of Calamity Connie. They printed a second one of Dapper Dallas.

"Okay, let's find the bandit," said Jessie. "We can start with Connie since she's in the saloon."

"Violet, you should be the one to ask for the autograph," said Henry.

Bart and Nellie stayed behind as the

children approached Connie. She was writing in a notebook. She looked up when the children arrived.

"Hello, kids," she said. "Good job finding those cattle! I bet your grandfather will be proud of you."

"Thank you," said Henry. "We wondered if you would do us a favor?"

"Sure," said Connie. "What's up?"

Violet showed Connie the photo of her. "Will you please autograph this for us?"

"Oh my, sure!" said Connie, laughing. "What would you like me to write?"

"Please have it read 'Calamity Connie at Wildcat Crossing,'" said Violet.

"Then we will always remember where we met you!" said Benny.

"Will do," said Connie. She reached for the photo and scribbled on the bottom. Then she handed it back. "How's that?" she asked.

Violet studied the autograph and smiled. "It's just perfect," she said. "Thank you so much, Calamity Connie!"

"You're very welcome!" she said. "I see you

also have a photo of Dapper Dallas. I saw him earlier at the museum."

"Yes," said Violet. "We want to get his autograph too."

"Here, take my pen," said Connie. "He probably doesn't have one."

The children thanked Connie and headed outside.

"Violet, you were smiling when you saw Connie's autograph," said Jessie. "Let's see!"

Violet showed her brothers and sister Connie's photograph.

"No swirly *r*," said Benny.

Henry pulled out the two notes. They compared more of the handwriting. "Her handwriting is nothing like the handwriting on the notes," said Henry.

"Calamity Connie is innocent," said Violet.

"Then the bandit must be Dapper Dallas," said Jessie.

The children walked down the road toward the museum just as Dapper Dallas was leaving the museum. He walked into the road and waved at them.

"There he is," said Benny.

"He sees us," said Jessie. "Let's keep going."

They walked toward Dallas as he walked toward them. Finally the children were face to face with Dapper Dallas.

"Hey, Aldens," said Dapper Dallas. "Good job today! You were a great help to us."

"Thank you," said Henry. "We enjoy being here."

"Violet has a favor to ask," Jessie said.

"Well, hello, little lady," Dallas said to Violet. "What favor would you like to ask?"

Violet shyly produced the photo of Dapper Dallas.

Dapper Dallas looked at the photograph. "I look terrific!" he said, smiling. "Can you send me a copy?"

"Yes," said Violet. "But would you please autograph this one for us?"

"Just give me a pen," said Dallas. Violet handed him Connie's pen.

"Please write 'Dapper Dallas at Wildcat Crossing,'" said Benny.

"I can do that," said Dallas, signing the

photo. Then he handed the photo and the pen back to Violet.

"Wow, look at that," said Violet. She showed the photo to Benny so he could see. Henry and Jessie looked over her shoulder.

"Look at what?" asked Dallas.

"You write a swirly *r*," said Benny.

"So?" asked Dallas. "I pride myself on my fancy handwriting!"

Henry pulled the two notes from his pocket. "Yes, you do," he said. "We noticed."

Dallas backed up a step, shaking his head. "What are those notes? I've never seen them. I never made any threats to Bart and Nellie!"

"What threats?" asked Jessie. "You just said you've never seen these notes."

"But you seem to know what they say!" said Benny.

Dallas sighed. "Oh okay, I give up," he said. "I didn't mean any harm by any of it."

"You put salt in the water tower? And hid Tricky Trigger?" asked Henry.

"Yes, that was me," said Dallas. He walked

to the wooden sidewalk. He plunked down on a wooden bench and hung his head.

"And you messed up the costumes? And turned the cattle loose?" asked Jessie.

"Guilty as charged," said Dallas. "But I had a good reason!"

"I'd like to hear that reason," said Bart. He and Nellie joined the children. Connie followed close behind.

"I figured if that Hollywood producer bought Wildcat Crossing, I'd get to be a real actor," said Dallas.

"Did they tell you to cause trouble?" Bart asked.

"Well, no, that was all my idea," said Dallas, shamefaced. "I'm really sorry. I just love acting so much. I guess I got all excited about being a real Hollywood actor."

"You are pretty good," said Bart. "The crowd loves you. But this was a terrible thing you did to Nellie and me!"

"I know, and I want to make it up to you," said Dallas.

"How will you do that?" asked Jack McCoy. He was standing behind Connie.

"You can have all my starring roles, Jack," said Dallas. "I'll take care of the horses and play all the bit parts. And I'll pay for the damages. Please, Nellie, Bart, give me another chance."

"Well, that might work," said Bart. "Assuming Jack can keep from being so dang bossy to everyone!"

Jack looked around and shrugged. "I never thought I was all that bossy," he said. "But I can work on that, I reckon."

"You're too easy on both of them, Bart," said Nellie. "Dallas, you'll also wash dishes for the rest of the festival. And, Jack, if you want to boss anyone, try to boss me. I dare you."

"Yes, ma'am, thank you, ma'am," both men said at once. They headed to the stable. Jack told Dallas he'd show him the ropes.

The children smiled, happy that things were working out. Then Violet noticed that Connie was walking back toward the saloon.

"Hey, Connie," Violet called to her.

Connie turned around. She was clutching the little notebook.

"I wanted to return your pen," said Violet. "Thank you for letting us borrow it."

"It's okay," said Connie. "I'm glad that you found our bandit."

"I wanted to ask you something," said Jessie. "Why were you out of breath just before we discovered that Trigger was missing?"

"Oh, did you think I had something to do with all of this?" Connie asked. She sighed. "I was out of breath because I lost track of time."

"What were you doing that was so important?" asked Nellie.

"I was writing songs in this notebook," said Connie. She handed the little book to her sister.

Nellie opened the book and leafed through the pages. "Wow, Connie, you have been doing a lot of songwriting."

"Music is my dream, Nellie," said Connie. "I love you and Bart and Wildcat Crossing, but I want to pursue my music career."

Nellie hugged her sister and patted her on the back. She looked at Bart and nodded. Bart headed back to the saloon without a word.

"Thank you, Aldens, for catching our bandit," said Nellie. "And thank you for helping me listen to my little sister. Let's go see about some supper."

They walked back to the saloon. Bart was inside, talking on the phone. He finished his call and smiled at everyone.

"I just talked to Jasper Beebe," said Bart.

"Oh no," said Jessie. "You didn't sell Wildcat Crossing after all, did you?"

"Heck no, Jessie," said Bart, laughing. "But Nellie and I had another idea."

"We figured since the festival is only once a year, maybe the Hollywood folks could lease the town some other time," said Nellie.

"But they have to honor history. That's the deal," said Bart.

"What did Jasper Beebe say?" asked Henry.

"He said they'd honor our wishes," said Bart. "He was very nice. He felt terrible about the pranks. He was glad you found the bandit."

"Leasing will earn us a little extra money,"

said Nellie. She smiled at Connie. "We'll give that money to you, for your dream."

"Thank you," said Connie. She hugged her sister.

"And by the way, Connie," said Bart. "Jasper said those Hollywood folks couldn't wait to see you perform."

Connie smiled and blushed.

"So we have to put on our best Wild West show ever," Bart continued. "Those Hollywood producers are coming to see us all perform!"

"Oh, don't tell Dapper Dallas," said Benny. "He'll want his starring roles again!"

"Dapper Dallas will be fine," said Bart. "I think he learned his lesson."

"We gave him another chance," said Nellie. "That's what we do in Wildcat Crossing."

"This is great news!" said Violet.

"It will be fun to see grumpy Jack McCoy in the starring roles," said Jessie. "I think he learned his lesson too."

"If not, we can call him Grumpy Jack!" said Benny.

Everyone laughed and headed to the saloon for supper. They had a lot of work to do to prepare Wildcat Crossing for Hollywood!

THE BOXCAR CHILDREN SPOOKTACULAR SPECIAL

created by Gertrude Chandler Warner

Three spooky stories in one big book!

From ghosts to zombies to a haunting in their very own backyard, the Boxcar Children have plenty of spooktacular adventures in these three exciting mysteries.

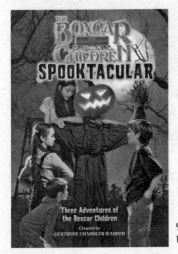

978-0-8075-7605-2
US $9.99 paperback

THE ZOMBIE PROJECT
The story about the Winding River zombie is just an old legend. But Benny sees a strange figure lurching through the woods and thinks the zombie could be real!

THE MYSTERY OF THE HAUNTED BOXCAR
One night the Aldens see a mysterious light shining inside the boxcar where they once lived. Soon they discover spooky new clues to the old train car's past!

THE PUMPKIN HEAD MYSTERY
Every year the Aldens help out with the fun at a pumpkin farm. Can they find out why a ghost with a jack-o'-lantern head is haunting the hayrides?

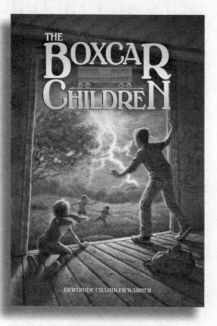

#1 THE BOXCAR CHILDREN
THE BOXCAR CHILDREN® MYSTERIES
HC 978-0-8075-0851-0
$15.99/$17.99 Canada
PB 978-0-8075-0852-7
$5.99/$6.99 Canada

"One warm night four children stood in front of a bakery. No one knew them. No one knew where they had come from." So begins Gertrude Chandler Warner's beloved story about four orphans who run away and find shelter in an abandoned boxcar. There they manage to live all on their own, and at last, find love and security from an unexpected source.

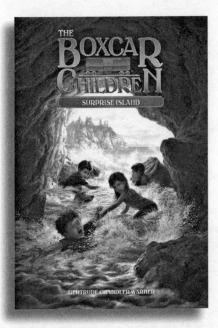

#2 SURPRISE ISLAND
THE BOXCAR CHILDREN® MYSTERIES
HC 978-0-8075-7673-1
$15.99/$17.99 Canada
PB 978-0-8075-7674-8
$5.99/$6.99 Canada
The Boxcar Children have a home with their
grandfather now—but their adventures are just
beginning! Their first adventure is to spend the
summer camping on their own private island.
The island is full of surprises, including a kind
stranger with a secret.

For more about the Boxcar Children,
visit them online at

TheBoxcarChildren.com

GERTRUDE CHANDLER WARNER discovered when she was teaching that many readers who like an exciting story could find no books that were both easy and fun to read. She decided to try to meet this need, and her first book, *The Boxcar Children*, quickly proved she had succeeded.

Miss Warner drew on her own experiences to write the mystery. As a child she spent hours watching trains go by on the tracks opposite her family home. She often dreamed about what it would be like to set up housekeeping in a caboose or freight car—the situation the Alden children find themselves in.

While the mystery element is central to each of Miss Warner's books, she never thought of them as strictly juvenile mysteries. She liked to stress the Aldens' independence and resourcefulness and their solid New England devotion to using up and making do. The Aldens go about most of their adventures with as little adult supervision as possible—something else that delights young readers.

Miss Warner lived in Putnam, Connecticut, until her death in 1979. During her lifetime, she received hundreds of letters from girls and boys telling her how much they liked her books.